THE LEGEND OF
Guava Bear

Written by Gale Bates
Illustrated by Carole Hinds McCarty

Dedication

To Mum

Love, G. B.

For Mom & Dad

Love, C. H. M.

Special Note

The Legend of Guava Bear is based on a true story.

In December 1956, a one-year-old American Black Bear cub escaped from his trainer's animal farm at Heeia-Kea on Oahu. First, the trainer set a trap by trying to lure him with a girl bear, but the bear only stopped to chat and never got close enough to catch. Then ten men from the 25th Infantry Division's land rescue search team made a search of nearby forests and mountains. However, because of the thick underbrush and his many hiding places, the clever bear always eluded them. His trainer told an interested public that he felt the bear was not in danger... "He is shy and gentle, but extremely clever and capable of taking care of himself." For the next 5 years, the bear was sighted by several people, but he always outwitted his hunters.

On the island of Oahu in Hawaii, there once lived a young, carefree American Black Bear. He lived on an animal farm in Nuuanu Valley at the foot of the Koolau Mountains and was a very clever bear who was trained to perform special tricks. He was gentle and funny and always made children laugh with his silly tricks.

Because he loved to eat sweet, juicy guavas, his friends called him Guava Bear. Every day he gazed at the lush tropical forest, dreaming of ripe yellow guavas. He would smack his lips just imagining the sweet, juicy taste of the guava's luscious pink filling.

One morning Guava Bear awoke and lazily stretched his arms, expecting to feel the familiar tug of his leash which was tied to a stake.

SNAP! The leash broke!

Guava Bear raised his eyebrows in wonder, then grinned as he looked across the yard at his little friend, Plumeria Bear, whom he called Plum. She was curled up near her stake, snoring softly.

"Hmmmmm...." he thought, "I can walk, I can skip, I can run, I CAN FIND GUAVAS!"

Chuckling happily to himself, he skipped across the yard to Plumeria.

"Plum! Plum! Look! My leash is broken!"

Plumeria sat up, rubbing her eyes. "Guava! What happened?"

"I don't know, Plum. I just did my morning stretch and the thing broke! Here, let me pull on YOUR leash. Then we can run into the forest and gather guavas!"

"No, no, Silly!" Plumeria exclaimed, "We can't go into the forest. It's too scary."

"Oh, come on, Plum. Let's go. It will be so much fun!"

"I can't, Guava, and you shouldn't either. Mr. Johnson will be mad!"

"I'm only going to find guavas. Ohhhh, I can taste them already!"

Plumeria sighed…"Well, if you must go, wear this lei po'o for good luck." She placed a plumeria lei on Guava's head and said, "Hurry back, Guava."

"You bet, Plum!" Then, with twinkling eyes, he waved and disappeared into the forest.

In the forest, Guava stopped here and there, looking for a sign that would lead him to guava trees. His super sensitive nose sniffed the air.

"Hmmmmm....Where are those guavas?" he grunted. Climbing a tree, he scanned the horizon.

"Yes!" he yelled when he spotted a bright yellow splash of color in the distance. Tumbling down the tree, he hurried in the direction of his favorite fruit.

"GUAVAS!" he bellowed and ran toward a nice sturdy tree with dozens of ripe yellow guavas hanging from the branches.

"At last!" he sighed, scooping up a large guava from the ground. Breaking open the fruit, he licked his lips over and over before swallowing the delicious guava pulp.

After a while, his tummy was full and Guava Bear felt tired. He lay down to rest on a bed of soft leaves in a nearby bamboo thicket.

"This is so comfy," he thought, "and so quiet." Soon he was fast asleep.

When he awoke some time later, he looked up at the beautiful moon shining through the bamboo. Yawning, he rolled over and thought how comfortable he felt in his new bed. Tomorrow he would return to the farm.

The next morning, he awoke and ate a breakfast of guavas.

"I wonder if there are more guava trees close by..." he thought. "It's time to explore!"

Over the next few days, Guava Bear was so happy in his new home. He spent his time searching the forest for guavas. He also found delicious blackberries and roots to eat. Each night he returned to his special bed of leaves in the bamboo thicket.

Then, one night, he heard a voice in the distance. He ran toward the voice and grinned when he recognized his little friend, Plumeria. She was tied to a stake at the edge of the forest.

"**Gu-ava Bear! Gu-ava Bear!**" Plumeria called, over and over.

Hiding behind a large hibiscus bush, Guava answered, "Over here, Plum!"

"Guava!" Plumeria whispered, "Are you alright? Why haven't you come home?"

"I'm having too much fun, Plum," he whispered back, "but why are we whispering?"

"Mr. Johnson is waiting for you, Guava Bear. He wants you back."

"Well, I don't want to come back, Plum. I like living in the forest."

"But aren't you scared?" Plumeria asked.

"No way! Why don't you join me?"

"Ohhh, no...." Plumeria said, as her eyes widened, "I'd be too frightened."

"There's nothing to be afraid of, Plum. Let's pull up your stake." He began to walk out from behind the hibiscus bush.

"No! No, Guava Bear! Keep out of sight!" Plumeria warned. "Mr. Johnson plans to follow you back to your hiding place and catch you when you fall asleep."

Guava Bear slipped back behind the bush. He was confused and disappointed.

"I'd better go, Plum. I'll be back to see you soon."

"Bye, Guava Bear," said Plumeria with a tear in her eye.

She worried about her friend being alone in the deep dark forest...and she missed him.

Guava Bear followed the secret pathway back to his special place in the bamboo thicket near his favorite guava grove.

Over the next few weeks, he roamed the Koolau Mountains forgetting about Mr. Johnson's plan to capture him. Near a new grove of guava trees, he found a bluff which overlooked a highway and he sat watching cars pass by. Feeling bored, he picked up two guavas and threw them in the air.

"Ah-HA!" he grinned. "I can still do that trick!"

He grabbed another guava. It dropped on the ground — SQUISH!

Gradually, he added another and another, and soon he was having a great time standing on the ridge juggling guavas.

The loud blast of horns disturbed his rhythm. He looked down to see motorists stopped on the highway, pointing at him. He bowed quickly and then fled back to the forest, fearing someone would tell Mr. Johnson.

Remembering Mr. Johnson made him think of Plum Bear. He gathered an armful of guavas as a gift for her and headed for the animal farm.

He saw Plumeria sleeping peacefully in the sunshine. Hiding behind a bush, he rolled the guavas one by one toward her.

Plumeria sat up, rubbing her eyes as a guava hit her in the back. Guava chuckled out loud. Smiling, Plumeria looked around, knowing who was nearby.

"Guava Bear, are you there?" she called softly.

"Of course, Silly," said Guava Bear. "Who else would throw guavas at you?"

"Well, stay where you are," Plumeria said. "Mr. Johnson is really getting upset because he can't find you. He's asked a search and rescue team to help him. Ohhhh.....Guava, I'm really scared for you."

"Don't worry, Plum," said Guava Bear. "No one can find my secret hiding place! I just wish you would come with me....."

"I cannot!" exclaimed Plumeria. "I'm too much of a scaredy cat. Are you really happy living in the forest?"

"Plum, it is the greatest place! I have enough food to eat and every day I find new and exciting places to visit. I'm even practicing some of my juggling tricks."

"*Shhhhh! Listen!*" warned Plumeria. "*Someone's coming! Quick! You'd better go!*"

Guava said a quick farewell to Plumeria and slipped back to the bamboo thicket.

The next day, while exploring, he discovered a banana plantation. He picked a ripe yellow banana from a hanging bunch. As he peeled away the skin, his nose began to twitch. A familiar smell caught his attention.

"HONEY!" he exclaimed. "I haven't had honey in sooooo long!"

Peering around the trunk of a banana tree, he spied a row of little boxes.

The smell of honey was stronger than ever. Carefully he stepped toward the little white boxes. Using his nose, he tried to open one of the boxes.

ZZZZZZZZZZZzzzzzzzzzzzz!

A swarm of bees flew around his head! Guava growled and tried to hit one with his paw.

Then he heard a loud shriek!

"AAAAAAAAYYYYYYYY!.......It's a BEAR!"

A lady by a nearby clothesline was pointing right at him. Even with all the buzzing around his head, Guava heard the lady shrieking some more.

All the buzzing and shrieking made his appetite for honey go away.

He turned and ran back along the ridges to his very secret place in the thick forest, and settled down for a nice long nap.

A loud whirring *chop! chop! chop!* sound woke him.

Curious, he climbed a tree to see what was making such a strange noise. From his perch, he saw men cutting their way through the underbrush.

Plumeria was right, he thought. Suddenly, the whirring sound grew louder and a large helicopter hovered near the trees. Guava Bear saw Mr. Johnson leaning out of the helicopter.

"There he is!" Mr. Johnson yelled.

Guava Bear ducked and grabbed a hanging vine. He swung to a large koa tree and clambered down. He wasn't frightened. He knew the search and rescue team and Mr. Johnson would not be able to find his place deep in the bamboo thicket. He ran to the ridge, but couldn't see anyone.

"**Grrrrrr!**" he growled loudly, but still, there was no one in sight. He shrugged his shoulders. "They're gone," he sighed. "Oh, well...."

Just then, two of the rescue workers appeared, covered up to their necks by the thick underbrush. He waved at them and ran back to the forest, darting in and out of the trees until he felt quite dizzy.

He tried to stand on his hands and walk upside down. With a loud THUMP, he landed on the ground.

"Over there! That's him!" He heard someone shout....

He laughed to himself and rested for a while. Everything became very quiet. Guava looked around. The searchers seemed to have disappeared, and the horrible noise of the helicopter was gone.

He strolled down to the stream and spotted two of the rescue workers filling their water bottles.

Poking his head around a tree, he uttered a long

"Grrrrrrrrrrrrrrr!!!!"

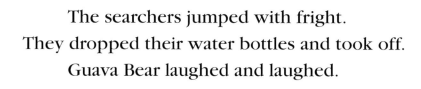

The searchers jumped with fright.
They dropped their water bottles and took off.
Guava Bear laughed and laughed.

He wondered if the searchers would return....

The search and rescue team can search for me, he thought, but I DON'T WANT TO BE RESCUED! I'm happy in the forest, hunting guavas! There's sooooo many guavas, I could spend years and years finding new groves, with bigger and BIGGER GUAVAS!

Sure, I miss Plum, and even Mr. Johnson, and I'll play surprise visits with them every now and then. But for right now, and tomorrow, and next year, and the year after that....

I'll have fun
finding guavas!

...and I'll have even more fun
EATING them!

...and so Guava Bear lived happily ever after in all his special guava groves in the Koolau Mountains...

Glossary

American Black Bear: Found on the North American continent, this large mammal has a massive body with coarse, heavy fur, relatively short limbs and a small tail. American black bears come in various shades of black, brown or tan and can weigh up to 300 pounds when fully grown. They eat most food, and are especially fond of fruit, berries, fish, insects and honey. Adult bears are happy being alone and can live to be 20 to 25 years old.

Guava: A small tropical tree from the myrtaceous family of the genus *Psidium*. Also, the berry like fruit from the tree. When ripe, it is yellow with a pink filling. The fruit is delicious and is used for making jam, jelly, juice, etc.

Oahu: The main island in the Hawaiian chain. Its capital is Honolulu.

Nuuanu Valley: A valley on the island of Oahu. It reaches up into the dense forest or center of the island.

Koolau Mountains: The main mountain range on the island of Oahu. Its largest peak has an elevation of 3,150 feet.

Plumeria: A fragrant waxy flower native to tropical America, the plumeria is the most loved lei flower in Hawaii.

Lei po'o: A lei or garland of flowers worn on the head.

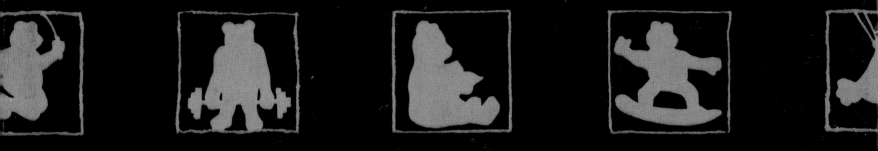